I0709031

ABOUT THE AUTHOR

Meet Mishica Moon, the beloved primary school teacher and children's author from London. As a child, she loved books and storytelling, which led her to pursue a career in education. Mishica's unique teaching methods and love for her students inspired her to write children's books that reflect their diverse experiences and contain important messages. She believes all stories have something to teach us. When she's not writing or teaching, Mishica advocates for education and literacy. Her books transport readers to magical lands and remind them of the magic in the world. Anything is possible with the imagination!

THANK YOU TO ALL THE AMAZING CHILDREN I'VE TAUGHT
FIRST PUBLISHED 2022 - WHERE IMAGINATION TAKES FLIGHT
NO PART OF THIS PUBLICATION MAY BE REPRODUCED, STORED IN A RETRIEVAL SYSTEM OR
The rights of Mishca Moon are to be identified as the author of this work
TRANSMITTED IN ANY FORM OR BY ANY MEANS, ELECTRONIC, MECHANICAL, PHOTOCOPYING, RECORDING OR OTHERWISE.

BANANA-TINE,
BE
MINE?

INTRODUCTION

In Bananaville, where yellow dreams shine,
A story unfolds, "Banana-tine, Be Mine?"
Benny's search for love, so sweet and fine,
Through vines and laughter, his heart inclines.

Grandbanana's wisdom, a fruity guide,
In Banana Blossom Park, love will abide.
With Pinky's smile, joy intertwined,
Banana-tine moments, one of a kind.

Under the moonlight, a banana dance,
In this tale of love, a charming chance.
So join the peel-ful fun, sweet and divine,
In the pages of love,
"Banana-tine, Be Mine?"

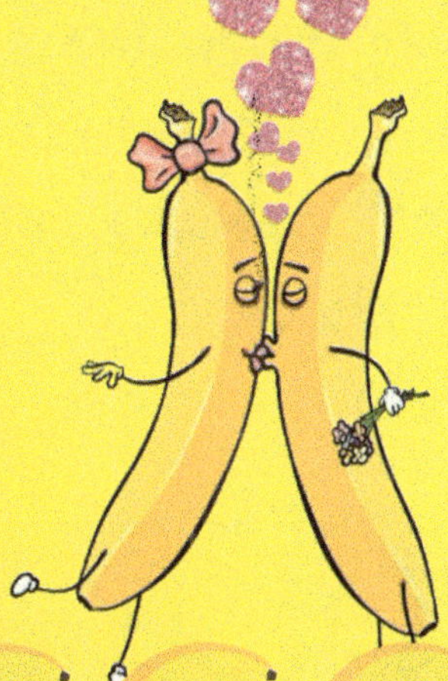

Once upon a time in the fruity town of Bananaville, there lived a banana named Benny. It was Valentine's Day, and Benny couldn't help but feel sad. As he strolled through town, he noticed all the Valentine's cards and balloons in a shop window. Benny, with a heavy heart, realised he didn't have a valentine to call his own.

CUPID'S CHUCKLE CHEST
Happy
Valentine's Day
LOVE
LOVE
LOVE
LOVE
Love you

As Benny turned the corner, he bumped into the wise old Grandbanana, who chuckled and shared a banana-ry joke to lighten the mood,
"Why did the banana go to the doctor? Because it wasn't peeling very well!"
Amused, Benny asked, "But Grandbanana, how do I find my valentine?"
Grandbanana, with a knowing smile, leaned closer and whispered, "Ah, young yella, love is like a banana—you can't rush the ripening. Stay positive, laugh a little, and trust that when the time is just right - divine timing, your valentine will peel into your life like the sunniest surprise!"
And with that, Benny felt a bit lighter, armed with wisdom and a giggle, ready to set out on his adventure to find the perfect valentine.

Hmmph!
When I was a young, slippery peel...

Benny embarked on his journey to work, his yellow peel practically glowing with hope. With a bounce in his step that could rival a jumping bean, he ventured into Banana Blossom Park, looking left and right, up and down, and even sideways like a curious crab on a Lanzarote beach—because, you know, love can be as tricky to spot as a sneaky snake in the grass.

As Benny meandered through the park, his heart thumped with anticipation, believing that somewhere in the tranqulity of the park, love was waiting to serenade him like a catchy banana tune.

-NUTTY COVE

Benny sauntered past the coconut smoothie stand, where the aroma of tropical delights filled the air. Suddenly, he bumped into his buddy Barry, a banana of wisdom and charm.

"Hey, Bazza!" Benny greeted, a twinkle in his eye. "I don't have a valentine. Can you help me find one?"

Barry, with a banana-split grin, put on his thinking peel. "Ah, Benny, my friend! Love is like pulling the skin on a banana; you've got to take it one delightful layer at a time. I can help you if you trust and have faith!"

Benny nodded, eager for Barry's banana-centric wisdom. Barry then whipped out a banana leaf and started jotting down tips and tricks for finding the perfect valentine.

"First," Barry began, "you must be as appeeling as a ripe banana. Smile and spread joy!"

Benny, with a sparkle in his eyes and a spring in his step, smiled at his wise friend. Barry, always ready to lend a helping hand (or peel, in this case), wore a grin stretching from ear to ear, just like a banana slice." and said, "Take a walk with me, my vitamin-rich friend, and we'll try to find you the perfect Banana-tine!"

With that, Benny and Barry set off on an adventure through the park, the gravel crunching beneath their peels like the beginning of Banana Boogie. As they strolled, Barry couldn't resist sharing a banana joke or two to keep the journey light-hearted. "What is a banana's favourite gymnastic move?
The splits!" he chuckled, leaving Benny in stitches.

The dynamic duo of banana buddies, Benny and Barry, strolled by the pond. Soon, their journey was ripe with excitement as they came across various bananas, each with a unique peelsonality.

First up, they stumbled upon the sweaty jogging banana, decked out in sporty sneakers and a soaked sweatband. He was preparing for a big date with his valentine. Curious and always up for a laugh, Benny asked, 'Why the rush, speedy banana?'

The jogging banana grinned and replied, 'I'm having a banana tart date, and I need to be in tip-top banana shape!' With that, he sprinted off. Benny and Barry chuckled at the sight, imagining a banana tart date. They continued their quest and soon bumped into the groove-loving banana, humming a fruity melody to the hipster banana, who sported a strange quiff and a twinkle in his eye underneath stylish glasses."

COOL!

After a couple of hours of the banana-tastic adventure,
Benny, the banana on a mission, found himself at a
crossroads. He had yet to discover his special Banana-tine
despite the fresh air, fruity laughter, and more banana puns
than he could peel. Feeling a tad blue, Benny bid farewell to
his pal Barry, who had banana-ry valentine plans of his own.
A burst of giggles caught Benny's attention as he continued
wandering through the enchanting surroundings. Suddenly,
Pinky, a banana with a smile that could outshine the sun,
waltzed over. Pinky, swinging a handbag like a fruity Mary
Poppins, said, "Hey Benny! What's bakin' in Bananaville?
Why the long face, my peely friend?" Benny sighed, "Oh,
Pinky, I was hoping to find my special Banana-tine, but it's
been slipperier than a banana skin on a water slide."
Pinky's eyes twinkled like dewdrops on a banana leaf as she
exclaimed, "Fear not, Benny! The Banana-tine of your
dreams is nearer than you think...

DON'T LITTER

Benny Boy! I've been watching you for a while and noticed you didn't have a valentine, so I made you a special Banana-tine card!" Pinky exclaimed, her cheerful voice echoing through the park like a melody of happiness. With a twirl and a hop, Pinky handed Benny a hot pink envelope with a glittery red heart that sparkled like a banana disco ball.

Benny's eyes widened with delight as he carefully opened the envelope, revealing Pinky's masterpiece of fruity artistry. The card featured a giggling banana surrounded by red hearts. The words were written in tall letters:

"I AM BANANAS FOR YOU!"

Benny couldn't help but grin from ear to ear, feeling as special as a classic Banoffee Pie with extra gooey toffee! "Oh, Pinky, you're the potassium to my heart! You're the sweetest peel in the bunch!" he exclaimed, giving Pinky a grateful banana hug.

Pinky beamed with pride, her smile brighter than an overripe banana in the sun. "I'm glad you like it, Benny!

I AM BANANAS FOR YOU!
HAPPY VALENTINES DAY!

Benny's eyes sparkled like tiny bubbles in a banana smoothie as he held the card. Unable to contain his excitement, he turned to Pinky.

"Banana-tine, Be Mine?" Benny asked a mix of anticipation and hope in his voice.

Pinky grinned from ear to ear with a blush that could rival a ripe strawberry.

"Absolutely, Benny! I'd love to be your Banana-tine!" she exclaimed, and the crickets erupted into a symphony of cheers.

Benny, overjoyed, twirled Pinky in a banana waltz, spinning like a fruity tornado.

Pinky's joy bubbled
like a fizzy fi...

...banana pop, and as she twirled
around her bedroom, she couldn't
decide what to wear for the Banana-
tine celebration. Should it be the pink
dress with the pink polka-dot boots?
Decisions, decisions!
After trying on outfits that ranged
from banana-chic to banana-glam,
Pinky decided to ask Barry.

Whoah, Pinky! You don't have to get dolled up. Just be YOU!

And just like that, Benny's Valentine's Day became a
day bursting with banana love!
Benny couldn't resist making a banana joke as they
swung on vines together.
"Why did the banana go to the jungle gym? To peel
some moves!" Pinky, giggling, added a banana pun
of her own, "What's a banana's favourite dance?
The banana cha-cha!"
They roasted banana marshmallows, told more bad
banana jokes, and kissed under the moonlight while
the stars twinkled with delight.
Feeling the banana love all around him, Benny
turned to Pinky and said, "Pinky, this has been the
best Banana-tine ever!
And so, under the glow of the moon, Benny and
Pinky, with their hearts as ripe as the sweetest
bananas, continued their Banana-tine adventure,
creating silly memories in Bananaville.

Soon, Benny and Pinky found themselves falling head over peels in love. The butterflies, always the first to sense love in the air, started humming banana love songs as they fluttered around the budding bananas.

With a look of love in his eyes and a banana bouquet in hand, Benny mustered up the courage to pop the big question. "Pinky, my sweet Banana-tine, will you be my forever snack?" he asked, holding out a banana-shaped engagement ring crafted from the finest banana leaves.

With a gasp of fruity delight, Pinky accepted the banana ring, and the butterflies erupted into cheers. The bishop, shedding a tear of joy, pronounced them the official Banana Couple of Bananaville.

As Benny and Pinky exchanged vows, promises of peeling each other's bananas and sharing ideas for banana desserts until the end of time, the butterflies erupted into laughter and pure joy.

And so, in front of a stunning stained-glass window, Benny and Pinky, now officially Mr. and Mrs. Peelworthy, danced their way into a lifetime of fruity love. The butterflies, still humming banana love songs, joined the celebration, creating a Banana-tine tale that would be retold and giggled about for generations in the heart of Bananaville.

I do
me too!

Also by Mishica Moon:
Bad Pig's Party
Mr Mousetivator
Unique Ulrika
King's Coronation Caper
Jiving in the Jungle
Jolly Harvest
Halloween Pals & Pumpkin Hugs
Adventures in the Arctic
Hugo's Christmas Hijinks
Maya's Magical Christmas
Goal Getters
Rise Up, Girl Power
Different, Yet One
and many more...